Also from Second Wind Publishing
Novels by Sherrie Hansen

Night and Day
Love Notes

Maple Valley Trilogy:

Book 1: *Stormy Weather*
Book 2: *Water Lily*
Book 3: *Merry Go Round*

Wildflowers of Scotland Series:

Wild Rose
Shy Violet
Blue Belle

www.secondwindpublishing.com

Thistle
Down

By

Sherrie Hansen

Beckoning Books
Published by Second Wind Publishing, LLC.
Kernersville

Beckoning Books
Second Wind Publishing, LLC
931-B South Main Street, Box 145
Kernersville, NC 27284

First Beckoning Books edition published
May 2013.
Beckoning Books, Running Angel, and all production design are trademarks of Second Wind Publishing, used under license.

For information regarding bulk purchases of this book, digital purchase and special discounts, please contact the publisher at
www.secondwindpublishing.com

Cover design by Tracy Beltran

Manufactured in the United States of America
ISBN 978-1-938101-49-6

To Mary Ann Olsen, for being a friend through good times and bad, and now, even better. I appreciate your encouragement and willing heart.

Chapter 1

"Two weddings in two months must be stressful for all concerned." Ian MacCraig reached behind his neckband, unbuttoned his clergy tab, and pulled it from his collar. He didn't mind wearing the contraption when he was in the pulpit, but the day had been long and his neck itched from being confined.

"Stress? Not at all," Edith Downey, the mother of the brides claimed. "Well, there was a little to-do about the date. Both girls had their hearts set on being June brides, and for various reasons, they chose the same weekend. I suggested that Emily should have first choice – she is the oldest. But then Chelsea started to cry..." Mrs. Downey had the grace to look chagrinned. "Chelsea really will be a good barrister once she's passed her bar examination. Ever since she was a little tyke, she's been adept at pleading her case."

No stress at all, Ian thought.

"But then Emily got mad and started in on me for spoiling the girl. I supposed I was a bit prone to letting Chelsea have her way when they were children."

"It's a natural thing, I suppose." He had only one sister, and he didn't even want to go there. He couldn't imagine the family dynamics that would come into play with five children.

"So Emily moved her wedding up to May?"

"Yes. I hope she's not rushing things, but who am I to say?"

"Is there some reason for concern?"

"Well, they've only known each other for four months. But Emily staunchly defends her reasons for wanting to get married."

Staunchly defends? Not, *'Emily's madly in love'*, or *'She's so head over heels with the laddie that she can't wait to be his wife'*? He made a note on his tablet.

"And what about Chelsea? How does she feel about her sister beating her to the punch so to speak?"

"Well, there's been the usual quibbling about Emily always

having to have the best, and worries that nothing Chelsea does will rival Emily's grand showing, but I just turn a deaf ear and hope it all goes away."

No stress at all, Ian thought again. "I'll look forward to meeting them all then."

"The girls will both be up tomorrow to celebrate my birthday, if you've time to see them on such short notice."

"Certainly." No reason he couldn't squeeze them in between the Nitters and Natters and his meeting with the Altar Guild. "We can take care of some of the logistics for the ceremony and use of the church, and schedule the pre-marital counseling sessions for each couple."

"Neither of them really needs counseling." Edith tugged at her hat.

"Not to imply that either couple is in need of my specific assistance, but it is part of the procedure for any couple I agree to marry."

"But they both grew up in this church."

"They were both grown and gone long before I came to St. Conan's. I haven't had the pleasure of meeting either of the men they're marrying. Taking inventory of their relationship styles and talking about anything that bears discussing is a good way to get to know each other. Even if they have the perfect relationships and have no need for counsel."

"I do understand. It's just that their schedules are so busy. Emily and Benjamin are both very mature. They're certainly old enough to know their own hearts. And they'd have to drive all the way from Glasgow."

She didn't say where Chelsea and Greg lived.

"Counseling is not an option. It's a requirement."

Edith remained quiet, but she did not look happy.

"I can concede that counseling may not be the most fondly anticipated part of getting married, but most couples do realize the wisdom in participating in the exercise."

Edith sighed, opened her mouth to speak, then closed it again.

"You can trust me to handle this, Edith. You've enough to do being mother of two brides."

"Yes."

"Leave it to me to win them over then. I'm sure we'll get on smashingly."

"Yes. Well. Better you than Reverend Stout."

Ian smiled. His predecessor had retired at the ripe old age of 87. "I do have the benefit of being about the same age as your daughters."

"Yes. Maybe they'll actually listen for once if it's coming from you." Edith laughed as though she was making a joke, but it was a hollow, half-strangled laugh that did not bode well.

"As I said, I'm sure we'll get on famously."

Edith left a few minutes later, still acting as though she'd signed on her daughters for the excision of impacted wisdom teeth instead of a few friendly chats about how to build a strong marital relationship.

Chapter 2

"I'll go first." Emily Downey was wearing a wool tweed jacket with a color-coordinated tam that matched her cool, composed, very self-assured aura.

"You always do." Chelsea Downey, who looked decidedly more frazzled in jeans with tattered pockets and a lace shirt, rolled her eyes.

"A right I've earned fairly." Emily frowned.

"What? For meritorious service earned in the line of duty?"

"I deserve a gold medal for tolerating my younger siblings."

"Just because you're the oldest-"

"And wisest."

Chelsea huffed and dropped the conversation, her attitude clearly indicating that her sister wasn't worth the energy it would take to continue the fight.

No stress at all. Ian felt a rush of sympathy for Edith Downey, and not for the first time. "Why don't we start with the exact times and dates you've chosen for your ceremonies?"

The brides-to-be rattled off the dates they'd each selected, declining to mention the reported drama that had surrounded their decisions.

Emily was all business. Chelsea had the look of a lovesick teenager. Both sisters had curly red hair and freckles, but that was where the similarities ended as far as Ian could tell.

"So tell me a little about yourselves and your beaus as well as what sort of time frame might work for your joint sessions."

"How many do we have to come to?" Emily looked irritated.

Her apparently equally disgruntled younger sister started to speak no more than a half-second after she finished. "Both Greg and I work full time, Saturdays, too. The only day of the week we have free is Sunday."

He'd hoped the women would go along peaceably so he wouldn't have to play the *required* card, but it didn't appear that was

4

going to happen. "Best to get the sessions over quickly then. I'm sure your weekends will only get busier as you near the dates of your weddings."

Both women looked at him as if trying to gauge the depth of his resolve and evidently resigned themselves to the inevitable.

"I'll have to check with Benjamin, but we could probably drive up next Saturday." Emily looked at her younger sister. "So you can have Sunday."

"How big of you." Chelsea agreed to speak to Greg, then went on to map out tentative dates for all three sessions. But she was still pouting when they were finished.

Truth be told, Ian wasn't wild about giving up a months worth of Saturdays and cramming one more commitment into his already exhausting Sunday schedule either, but no one seemed to appreciate his sacrifice. That said, pre-marital counseling sessions ranked high on the list of the pastoral duties he enjoyed most. Talking to prospective brides and grooms, no matter their age or situation was infinitely more fun than dealing with the aftermath of a death or divorce, and much more challenging and rewarding than sitting with the ladies at Missionary Society or their weekly quilting sessions. He'd always preferred proactive measures to reactive, and counted the task of equipping couples for a long, happy partnership to be a great honor.

"So, tell me a little about the men you'll be marrying."

"I'm sure once you meet Benjamin, you'll agree that he'll be the perfect husband." Emily raised an eyebrow in Chelsea's direction.

Chelsea responded with a huffy, "And you'll see how deeply in love Greg and I are."

Ian looked from one sister to the other. Was Chelsea trying to imply that Benjamin and Emily weren't marrying for love? Come to think of it, he didn't recall the word being mentioned by either Emily or her mother. It would be very interesting to meet Benjamin.

"What does Benjamin do? And Greg? How long have you known one another? Any previous marriages or children from prior relationships that I should know about?" He'd wait to ask the more personal questions – whether or not the couple was having pre-marital sex, or even living together, what their points of contention were, how they communicated, if they agreed on how to spend money – when he was alone with each couple. Some of it would be covered in a questionnaire he'd send home with the women, to be filled out by each individual in the relationship and placed in a sealed envelope, for his eyes only.

Once again, Emily spoke first. "Benjamin is a doctor. A cardiologist." Her tone was almost gloating. "We've known each other since last December."

It was left to him to do the math. Emily obviously knew the public relations business well, as she should, since it was her career. December of last year sounded infinitely longer than the mere four months it had actually been. He made a note for his file. Based on what he knew from friends who'd pursued medicine as a career, there were probably no prior relationships – the poor chap most likely hadn't had a moment to himself in all the time he'd been in school, residencies and internships.

"Chelsea?"

Chelsea squirmed and fidgeted in her chair. "Greg is, well, um, Greg is, well, I'm not sure which of his jobs he would consider his actual career."

Emily rolled her eyes. Chelsea, who was sitting beside her and focused on Ian, didn't notice.

"Why don't you start with the one he enjoys the most."

A smile lit up her face. "He loves playing with his band, and writing music – they play old time rock and roll. Like the Beatles and the Monkees, plus their own stuff. And they're really, really good. It's just that, by the time they divide their earnings between the four of them, and buy the equipment they need and transport everything to the gigs they get – well, he just doesn't make that much being a musician. But he's really, really wonderful at it, and he's got so much talent that I support his efforts to make it in the music business 100%. And someday, I'm positive he's going to get a break and..."

A definite worry. But Ian couldn't help but smile at her enthusiasm. "He has a second job?"

"He's a bartender at the Bump and Grind, which is a really nice, upscale pub on Barrie Street, if you're at all familiar with Dumbarton. He can get more hours if he needs to, but that would mean working weekends, and that's when his band is usually playing, so..."

Chelsea glanced at Emily, and then back at him, her eyes

pleading with him to let it drop. Judging by Chelsea's nervousness, he could probably guess the answer to his questions about previous relationships or children. And that's why he nodded reassuringly instead of asking.

"And we've been together for three years." It was Chelsea's turn to flaunt it now, and she did. "We've just been waiting because, well, we wanted to save up some money before we..., and wait until I'd graduated from law school before..."

"I understand," Ian said. Both relationships were obviously more complicated than Edith had led him to believe. And it was clear that he needed to stop asking questions until he had each of them one on one.

He stood and smiled. "Thank you so much for coming by today, then, ladies. I've got a packet for each of you with the questionnaires I mentioned on the mobile, and directions on how to fill them out. Please call to confirm your next appointment once you've had a chance to speak to Benjamin and Greg, and hopefully, we'll see you both weekend after next."

Emily pursed her lips and resumed looking smug.

Chelsea looked visibly relieved. "We're done then? Because Greg is waiting for me out in the car."

Emily was the first to stand and shake his hand. Chelsea followed suit.

They both started to exit. But instead of going first, Emily hung back and let Chelsea walk out ahead of her.

"He's got two – that we know of," Emily whispered as soon as Chelsea had walked far enough to be out of earshot. "Charlie is two. Gretchen is a year and a half. Da and Mum don't know."

Chapter 3

The winds were blustery and cold and the snow was flying sideways, but the stone spires of St. Conan's didn't flinch or waver one iota. Just a few days earlier, they'd had a stretch of wonderfully warm weather. The grass had greened up, buds had burst open, and the air had been so warm that Ian had even thought about taking a picnic under the flying buttresses.

Then winter had made a comeback. *Crazy spring weather.* He'd assumed the roads might be slippery, so he was surprised to see Emily Downey walk in the door. Alone.

"Hello, Emily." He jumped to his feet and greeted her with a handshake. He was grateful she'd come. It showed resolve and commitment on her part. Perhaps Benjamin was parking the car – if not, that was fine. Today was to have been about bonding, and he hoped that without the tensions that had been present at their last meeting, it could begin, if not with the couple, then at least with the bride.

"I'm so sorry that Benjamin couldn't be here." Emily swiped her hair away from cheeks pink from the cold wind blowing off the loch and unbuttoned her coat. "One of his patients had a heart attack so he couldn't leave town. It was either cancel or come by myself and I figured, given the line of work that my future husband is in, I might as well get used to doing things on my own."

She didn't seem rattled in the slightest, or even disappointed, which Ian thought a little odd. But there were certainly things the two of them could discuss without Benjamin being there.

She settled into the old leather chair opposite his desk and smiled up into his eyes.

He blinked, taken aback by the intensity of her gaze. "So where shall we start?"

"Wherever you like is fine with me."

He thought for a moment. "If I may, I'd like to ask you what attributes first attracted you to Benjamin? And what about the way you think of him now? How have your feelings changed in the four months since you first met?"

"Benjamin is good and kind, honest, and extremely intelligent. He's passionate about his work and highly respected in his field."

The string of exceptional qualities that continued sounded more like a line by line listing on a resume, more like a business arrangement than a love story, but he tried to be respectful and listen.

"And how has your relationship grown since you met Benjamin?" He didn't use the word love because she hadn't.

"I don't think it has. We're both the kind of people who are very stable, solid, and purposeful. We know our own minds, and when we met, we both saw in the other exactly the kind of person that we'd been looking for and desired in a spouse."

He wanted to ask her if she believed in love at first sight, if she even loved the man, if her perfect fiancé had ever once claimed to love her. He wanted to ask her if she would even be considering getting married in May if her youngest sister hadn't announced her own engagement. But he didn't. He bided his time.

"Is there anything that you don't like about Benjamin?"

"Would I be marrying him if there was?"

"That's a good question. Because, I'm here to tell you that despite all his wonderful qualities, your fiancé is not perfect. Given the short time that you've known one another, the thing that will grate on your nerves may not have made itself apparent – yet – but it will."

"Of course," she said, as if realizing that the picture she had painted was too perfect to be believable. For a second, she looked flustered. And then, she did what any experienced PR person would – she put a positive spin on things.

"That's the magic, then, isn't it? Each day we're together will be full of new discoveries. Never a dull moment – that's how we both like to live our lives. So we're a good fit in that respect, too."

"Good." He hadn't expected her to break, not yet. It was a dance, getting to the truth, developing the trust necessary to bare one's soul.

He dialed it back a notch. "So I understand that Chelsea and you are the last two of your siblings to be married."

"Well, Chelsea will be. The last of us to marry, I mean."

"So, tell me about your other brothers and sisters. What kind of marriages do they have?"

She looked flustered again. She hadn't anticipated this question.

"I'm the oldest, as I'm sure you know. My sister, Kara, is a year and a half younger than me. She was the first to marry, the first to have children." Emily smoothed her skirt. "We're very different, she and I. She had no desire to go to college or see the world. She married her high school sweetheart. They seem happy – I mean, he makes her happy. I've never quite understood it, but I respect her for knowing what she wanted and having the courage to follow her dream."

"And your brothers?"

"Michael has been married for about two years now. His wife is nice enough. She's expecting their first baby in April. Matthew and Melissa's wedding was a year ago now, but they're still acting like they're on their honeymoon. What can I say? Young love..."

"Are you sorry you never had-"

She laughed. "Relieved is more like it." Her face turned serious. "When I look at Chelsea – I mean, she's a smart girl when it comes to everything but Greg. He walks into the room and she's brainless. If that's what kind of fool love makes of a person, I'm better off without it."

"So you're so afraid of appearing foolish that you're ready to enter into a loveless marriage to avoid the possibility of losing control?" Now they were getting down to the truth.

"That's not what I said." She was riled, which was exactly what he wanted, wasn't it? To make her think, to get her to feel.

"And Benjamin loves me dearly, so our marriage will hardly be loveless." She still hadn't said that she loved him. "I'm not sure if you've ever met my oldest aunt, Patricia MacDougall. Her son, Torey, is a professional golfer. They moved to Ayr several years ago, probably in part because of what happened the day Torey was to have been wed. I was ten or eleven years old. I can still remember how Torey looked, standing at the front of St. Conan's in his kilt, waiting for his bride to walk down the aisle. It was like a fairy tale, really. She was as beautiful as a princess. All I remember about her was that her name was Mary Ann."

"What happened?"

"She left him standing there. It was horrifying. He cried. A grown man. I can't even imagine the humiliation. He really loved her, you know?"

"I can only imagine."

"Pastor Ian? Or may I just call you Ian?"

"Certainly." She was giving him the same intense look she had when they'd begun their session.

"I don't mean to offend you, but I just need to know that you'll not repeat anything that's been said here to Chelsea, or my mother, or my Aunt Margaret, or anyone else who may know me..."

"You have my word."

"Thank you." She put on her coat and got ready to brave the winds once more.

"I'll look forward to speaking with Benjamin next week."

A look of surprise flashed across her face. "Yes. Of course. Of course you'll meet him."

"I'm sure he's a fine gent."

She left a few seconds later.

Chapter 4

When Ian heard the massive doors that led to St. Conan's inner sanctuary creaking open, he assumed it was tourists come to check things out – a common occurrence on Sunday afternoons. Although the curious stares and gawking admirers of St. Conan's gothic architecture weren't always a welcome interruption, it was their donations that more often than not paid the bills, and he welcomed them heartily for that reason.

He was expecting Chelsea and Greg, but not until half past two. He'd hoped the pair would have attended church services and met with him directly afterwards. But Edith and Emily had been the only two from the Downey family to come to church. Emily had been surprisingly chatty, and her mother, just the opposite. Edith had passed along some excuse about Greg not feeling well enough to attend and a quick reassurance that Chelsea was sure he would be quite all right by mid-day. Ian doubted Greg was truly ill, having read the sketchy comments Greg had filled in on the personal inventory he'd asked each couple to complete and put in the mail.

So two hours later when Emily Downey poked her head round the corner of the vestibule where his office was located, he was surprised to say the least.

But not as surprised as he was when she hugged him.

"Oh, Ian, I was ready to go home to Glasgow and then I started thinking about what we talked about yesterday and couldn't bear the thought of leaving until I'd thanked you for everything you've done for me." She snuggled her head against his chest and wrapped her arms around his neck.

Wow. He'd not seen this coming. He disengaged her arms as gently as he could and held her at arm's length. Had she had some sort of breakthrough? Was she being sincere?

"I just wanted to talk to you a little longer." Emily's eyes were soft, gentle, and sincere. "I hope you don't mind my dropping by."

"Of course not."

"No one has–" Emily faltered over her words, her emotions hidden no longer, but perched on the very surface of her body. "It's been a long time since anyone has cared enough to take the time to find out what I think and feel."

"It's a busy world we live in," Ian said. "I'm afraid I'm guilty of doing the same to my family, and those I love most. I've always found it interesting – the fact that speaking directly about matters of the heart comes so naturally here, with relative strangers, when it is so difficult in our daily lives, with those whom we are close to."

"I knew you would understand," she said, missing his point, and making him feel even more uncomfortable.

"I've been thinking a lot since yesterday, and I think I've discovered something about Benjamin that does bother me just a wee little bit."

"Okay."

Emily stared at him soulfully.

"Go ahead."

"Well, it's just that, when we talk - I mean Benjamin and I – I can hardly get a full sentence out without his mobile ringing, or a text message coming in about this patient or that, or a nurse needing his opinion, or another doctor paging him for a consultation. I know he's not doing it on purpose, and I know he's terribly interested in what I have to say, but it's just so distracting."

"I can see why that might be irritating."

"Yesterday, I mean, the way you and I were able to talk on and on, just the two of us, the conversation flowing from one topic to another, and me having your full attention, without a single interruption for over an hour... I just felt so cared about, and appreciated, and... loved."

Ian cleared his throat. Assuming he was reading her correctly, he had a problem. "Well, really, I think it's the whole experience of being at St. Conan's that probably affected you so deeply. I talk to dozens of people, hundreds really, and it's always the same. The architecture here is just so stunning. People are constantly telling me that the way the light filters through the stained glass windows and the lofty feeling of the Gothic ceilings paired with the cozy feeling of the chancel archways gives them an exquisite sense of well-being. So truly, it's nothing to do with me personally, rather God stirring those who seek His spirit."

"But I felt that you and I also connected on a very intimate level," Emily said, not catching on.

"Well, then, if this is about communicating more effectively, I have some exercises you and Benjamin can use to enhance your conversations." Ian swiveled round to his file cabinet and flipped through his folders.

"It's not just about the way things are when Benjamin and I are talking," Emily said. "It's our whole lifestyle."

Ian turned and looked at her again. It would be rude not to.

"Generally speaking, I love my life and my career in public relations. I enjoy the hectic pace, being constantly busy, rushing from one thing to another, and the feeling of having my intellect and reflexes stimulated. But every once in awhile..."

"Yes?"

"Well." She blushed. "There are times when I can see leaving it all behind and settling right here in Lochawe, living in a wee little stone cottage in the glen and raising a family just the way my Mum did."

Ian took a deep breath and forged on. "I'm sure the people of Lochawe would love having a doctor nearby, even if only for a few days a week. But if Benjamin shares your dream of living in the country, he would probably have to change his specialty to general medicine, assuming cardiologists need to practice out of a sizeable medical center and not a country clinic."

"Oh, I didn't mean... I'm quite sure Benjamin would lose his mind if he had to live in Lochawe."

"But..."

"See, that's the thing about committing to a lifetime with Benjamin. It's more than a pledge to the man, it's adopting that entire busy, big-city lifestyle for all eternity. And I just don't know if..."

He was about to say, 'But when you love a man,' and then he remembered that she probably didn't.

"Then you must be honest with Benjamin about your concerns."

"But that's the thing. I may be able to share my thoughts and fears with you, but there's no way I could have this conversation with Benjamin."

"That's also very natural. There's a lot at stake when it comes to Benjamin. Perhaps you're afraid of hurting him, or that he'll feel disillusioned with your relationship if he knows you're unhappy."

"Yes, I suppose that's possible. But I think part of it is his personality. You're so different than he is. You're laid back and compassionate and..."

He stood without even realizing he was going to do it – probably his fight-or-flight response kicking in. He saw his mistake as soon as she followed suit, stepped closer, and hugged him again.

He'd been trained in how to handle the woes of transference in his counseling classes, but never had he actually had to deal with it. Perhaps he was overreacting, but unfortunately, he didn't think so.

"Well, thank you for that." He loosened her arms from their new perch at his waist and stepped back a good two feet. "And now, best be on your way. Chelsea and Greg should be here any moment."

Her eyes took on a tortured look. "Yes, I should be going. Benjamin phoned and suggested that we have dinner together this evening – to make up for not being able to come to Loch Awe with me as planned."

"A very thoughtful gesture."

"Yes." She gazed at him soulfully.

He stepped towards the door and motioned to the exit with his right arm.

"I'll be on my way then."

"Until next week," Ian said, doing his best to look aloof.

Chapter 5

Emily had no sooner driven onto the main road when a small, battered car entered the lot. Chelsea was driving, and from the way Greg was slouched in the seat beside her, it was apparent that he wasn't pleased to be there.

Ian watched from the door of the chapel as they climbed from the car. No trying to be nice from this one. Greg was an exceptionally good-looking man with longish blond hair, broad shoulders, a lean, muscular body, and a stylish goatee, yet the expression on his face was very unbecoming. Chelsea hung not only on his arm, but on his every word. Even from a distance, the loyalty between them was palpable.

"I don't see why we have to get married here," Greg said, emphasizing the word *here* like it was dirty.

Neither of them seemed to realize that the wind was carrying their words to Ian.

Chelsea laughed nervously. "I've dreamed of walking down the aisle of St. Conan's since I was a wee lassie. Plus, it would mean a lot to my mum and da if we get married here. It's where most - if not all - of the people who care about me are."

"Did you ask him about doing a civil ceremony instead of a religious one then?"

"Not yet, but I will," Chelsea said, still not realizing Ian could hear every word they were saying.

Greg looked up and caught his eye. Oh – he knew.

The whole exchange was a probably a microcosm of what lay ahead - Greg manipulating Chelsea into doing it his way, Greg acting fragile so that Chelsea would turn her back on what she wanted and believed in and give in to him lest he grow disgruntled or tired of her and leave.

Ian took a deep breath. Whereas Emily's situation was slightly disconcerting, Chelsea's was infinitely more complicated. At best, the woman was letting her love blind her to reality, at worst, their relationship had the markings of an abusive one. He would have to tread lightly and choose his words carefully. It was possible Greg could be redeemed – as long as he was present and at least pretending to listen. If Greg left, or refused to come back, Ian's chance would be lost.

He nodded at Chelsea like nothing was amiss and reached out his hand to Greg. "Nice to meet you."

Greg's hand was hot and damp, his grip, weak.

"If we can do what we have to do and get out of here early, that would be great. I have a gig tonight."

"Okay. Let's step inside and talk about your answers to the questionnaire I sent home with Chelsea." He smiled.

"What? Do we get graded?" Greg laughed. Chelsea did, too.

"There are no right or wrong answers. The questions are designed to stimulate conversations about topics you may need to discuss before marriage, or to bring your attention to areas where you may have differences that need to be resolved - or at least acknowledged."

"Whatever." Greg grumbled. Chelsea giggled nervously.

Ian wanted to avoid the subject of Greg's indiscretions until they'd developed some sort of rapport, but he also wanted to be taken seriously, not mocked.

He needed safe ground. "How about we start by talking about the wedding? Chelsea, you go first, please. Tell me how you envision your wedding day, where you'd like to spend your honeymoon, and what you imagine your first week of married life with Greg will look like. Greg, you'll have your chance when Chelsea is done, so while she's talking, I'd like you to listen, but not speak. Are you okay with that?"

"I guess so."

"Thanks. Chelsea? Whenever you're ready."

Chelsea looked at Ian, glancing sideways at Greg every so often, her fear still apparent in her voice. "I've always dreamed of a traditional wedding. You know – a white dress with a full skirt and a train, and kilts for the men, and bridesmaids and flower girls and a big ceilidh afterwards." She turned to Greg. "But if that's not what you want, I'm flexible. It should be what both of us want."

Greg looked unfazed. It wasn't as though he couldn't give her what she wanted. He simply didn't care.

"Greg will have his chance later, Chelsea. Right now, we just want to hear your thoughts."

"Well, I guess it would be fun to go on a real honeymoon – I mean, if money were no object, and if we could do whatever we wanted."

"Go ahead," Ian said.

"It's just that I've been working so hard to pass my bar examination, and studying such long hours. And now, the wedding." She looked at Greg, visibly seeking his approval, finding none. "Wouldn't it be fun to go someplace exotic like Greece or the Italian Riviera, or Monaco? You know, someplace where we've always dreamed of going, just the two of us."

"It's okay, Chelsea. How do you envision your life when you come home from the honeymoon?"

She glanced shyly at Greg. "Well, I've always dreamed of a little stone cottage with blue shutters and a door with a round top. And window boxes and a garden with a pretty gate."

"Right," Greg said. "The motor home isn't good enough for you all of the sudden?"

"That's not it at all." She shrugged her shoulders and cocked her head in Ian's direction. "He said I should say what I wished for, not what is. I know we can't afford a house. Not until I pass my exams and get a job."

"Houses tie you down." Greg looked more and more exasperated. "You get a house, and suddenly you can't accept a gig on the weekend because you have to stay home and clean it, or mow the lawn, or weed the garden, or fix the roof, the front steps or the rusty gate. And if you don't, your wife is bitching at you and you're screaming at her and... Houses ruin everything."

Chelsea's eyes opened wide. Greg's feeling bitter about the two of them having a home was obviously news to her.

Which was a very good thing – of course Ian felt bad that Chelsea was having a rude awakening, but better now than after the wedding.

He looked at the *happy* couple and tried to decide whether or not to keep pressing. It might be better to drop things here and let them continue on their own when they'd each had some time to process. Chelsea already looked quite devastated, and Greg, like he was about ready to lose it.

"You've really done quite well, then," he said after a few moments of silence. "It's good to get your feelings out in the open."

"Right," Greg said.

"Anything you'd like to add, Greg?"

"Since you asked..." Greg practically sneered at him.

"Go ahead."

"I wouldn't even be getting married if it wasn't so important to Chell. I sure as hell wouldn't be getting hitched in some musty old kirk."

"Okay."

"My ideal honeymoon would be not having to go to my stinking job for a couple of weeks, but I can't afford to take the time off, so the best I've got is to tell the guys in the band to get lost so we can have the caravan to ourselves for a few hours."

"As for the rest, I don't bother dreaming about the future and what wonderful things might be in store for me because it's never gonna happen anyway."

Unlike her intended, Chelsea had remained silent during Greg's discourse. She was probably in shock.

"Anything you'd like to say to Greg, Chelsea?"

"No."

"Let's talk about our next session then." Ian felt like he needed to give Greg a specific reason to come back, or it was likely he'd have no further chances to spur the man on to greater things.

"Greg, Chelsea tells me you're an excellent musician. For next week, I'd like you to write a song that describes how you feel about being married to Chelsea."

Greg looked surprised. "Sure. I mean, whatever."

Chelsea, probably wisely, said nothing, but she looked at Ian gratefully.

A few minutes later they were gone, and Ian was left to ponder what had transpired. He wasn't even sure what his objective should be – to urge caution, to recommend that they delay getting married until they were both a little more ready, or to give in to what was probably inevitable and do everything he could to foster growth in both of his immature, misguided charges.

Chapter 6

Unlikely as it was, Ian was looking forward to a quiet day. Many pastors took Mondays off to recover from the stresses and business of the weekend. The tradition at St. Conan's was for the women of the church to quilt on Mondays, followed by a once weekly cleaning on Tuesdays to cover in one fell swoop any needed maintenance following the cumulative damage from any special events held on Saturday, Sunday services, and Monday's activities.

Thankfully, the women more or less took care of themselves, the telephone was usually quiet, and since many people and most of his peers assumed he had Mondays off, he rarely had visitors.

The quilters had promised freshly made caramel shortbread to start off the day, so he rose bright and early, showered, dressed, and headed next door to the kirk.

The first thing he heard was, "Well, you know now!" followed by Edith's tearful voice countering, "But what am I to do about it? She loves the laddie. Nothing any of us has said has made a whit of difference so far. She takes after her Granny Downey, that one."

"Stubborn as a mule," someone else said. "I remember the woman well."

"I had no idea," Edith said, blotting her eyes just as he leaned around the corner. "Does he see the children? Share custody? Will Chelsea be expected to feed and clothe them? Am I to treat them like grandchildren? Oh, my poor baby."

Ian stepped back into the shadows of the massive beams that framed the doorway from the chancel to the nave.

"And while she was seeing him, too. If he's been unfaithful to her twice in as many years, who's to say it will ever stop?"

"You can guarantee it willnae," Margaret said.

"Oh, my poor baby!" Edith wailed again.

"We have to do something. We can't just sit on our bahookies and watch the girl throw her life down the crapper."

"We've all known scoundrels like this Greg whomever he is. We can't stand by and let him ruin Chelsea's life."

He was just ready to announce his presence when he heard one of the ladies say, "What about Pastor Ian? He's as fine looking as her Greg is, and has a heart o'gold to go with the pretty face."

"What a wonderful idea!"

"Why didn't I think of that?"

"Didn't Pastor Ian consider going into law when he was younger?"

"See how much they have in common?"

"He is a wee bit older than she is."

"He's closer to Emily's age, isn't he?"

"But Emily already has a good man. It's Chelsea who needs our help."

"They've already met," Edith said. "Chelsea and Greg were in for counseling just yesterday."

Put a stop to it right now, he told himself, trying to convince his feet to move. But they appeared to have grown roots and planted themselves in the solid stone floor.

"Then the seed has been planted. How could anyone sit in a room with Pastor Ian MacCraig and that louse of a man and not see who was the better catch?

Get in there right now and put an end to it. Pure nonsense.

"Did she say anything after the meeting? Any comments about how good-looking Pastor Ian is, or what a good listener he is, or how considerate he is of other people's feelings?"

He peeked around the corner to see who was saying such nice things about him. It was flattering that they thought so kindly of him, even though their scheme was utterly ridiculous.

"Now that she's met Pastor Ian, I can't imagine she'd still be interested in that jerk Greg."

"If only things were that simple," Edith lamented.

There was a slight pause in the conversation whilst they evidently considered the complexity of life. He was just inching his foot forward when another unidentifiable voice took up the refrain.

"How did you find the dirt on this Greg anyway?"

"He's friends with my oldest daughter on Facebook."

"I thought he was homeless? How can he afford a computer?"

"Practically homeless. The members of his band all live in a caravan. No one knows quite where they're parked at any given moment."

"One little camping car for the whole lot of them? Won't that be cozy after the wedding."

"And they all have mobile phones."

"Isn't that the way it always is? The more assistance they get from the government, the fancier the tablet."

"Isn't he afraid Chelsea will find out what he's up to?"

"Poor thing is always so busy studying for her classes, and now, her Professional Competence Course and her provincial bar examination, that she doesn't have time for social media."

"From what I hear, it wouldn't make any difference what this Greg says on Twitter or Facebook or anywhere else. Everyone says that Chelsea is so smitten with the laddie that she'd not walk away from him no matter what he did."

"So ye're sure she knows about these children he's fathered with other women?" Edith asked again.

"Yes. At least she knows the women claim Greg is the father. And from what I've seen on Facebook, the one little laddie looks just like him."

"Who knows what Greg has told her? Lying goes hand in hand with sneaking around and always has."

"Ye cannae have one without the other."

"But she's such a smart girl," Edith said. "How can she not see it?"

"She's not the first woman to be sucked into a toxic relationship by a silver-tongued devil like Greg."

"It'll have to be up to you to stress Pastor Ian's finer qualities to Chelsea, Edith."

Someone snorted. "Stress? The girl has eyes, doesn't she?"

"Don't be too obvious," a familiar voice recommended. Probably Bertha Cleary. "Just a hint here and there to water the seed."

"That seed of yours better be one that germinates pretty quickly. We don't have much time."

He was just ready to walk into the room and put an end to their silly notions when he heard his mobile ringing from afar. He must have left it on his desk.

The ladies would have to wait. He tried never to let his telephone ring unanswered in case someone was calling with a pastoral emergency.

He followed the ring tone and rushed to grab his mobile. When he discovered it was the church's insurance agent on the line, he was almost disappointed that no one was calling to report a crisis - especially once he'd learned the reason for the call.

He sighed with frustration. "So you're saying that our insurance will go up by forty percent unless we raise our deductible to 10,000 pounds."

"You'd still have adequate coverage in the event something catastrophic should occur," his agent was quick to assure him.

"But any petty instances would have to be handled by the congregation?"

"If you stop and think aboot it, there's rarely such a thing as a small fire, or a wee bit o' flooding. If something's going to happen at a property as old as and the size of St. Conan's, it's going to be a major occurrence. And as far as the rest – well, your liability coverage will stay intact, and – who would steal from a church?"

"I guess we do have a certain amount of inherent protection from most occurrences of that sort."

"It's not like you're down in Glasgow or over in Edinburgh. If you can't trust the folks in your neighborhood, then what have ye got?"

"The Lord is good to watch over us."

"A built-in, protective hedge of prayers hovering round the whole kit and caboodle."

"I suppose we have no choice," Ian said.

"Well, now that you mention it, St. Conan's is already almost half a year behind with their premiums. It'll all be a moot point if they don't bring the account up to speed and soon. Ye have to do what ye can to trim down your expenses without sacrificing your liability coverage."

"I understand. I'll phone round to the members of the Kirk Session this evening and see what they recommend."

"I'd be scheduling a work day while you're at it. Our annual inspection of the property revealed a great deal of dangerous underbrush surrounding the property. There's also a broken step that's an accident waiting to happen."

"The rhododendrons and the wild roses do need to be trimmed back."

"There's a lot of recent deterioration of the outside structure, and loose, crumbling rock on the steps and walkway around the flying buttresses on the back side of the building."

Ian knew what the man was saying was true. It had been a roller coaster ride of a winter and the constant freezing, thawing and refreezing had taken its toll on the old rocks that comprised the steps, pillars, and walkways along the loch. The church had employed a full time groundskeeper until the previous fall, when budget cutbacks had necessitated the elimination of the position. Volunteers were the key they relied upon to take care of such things now, but while their intentions were good, rounding people up to actually do the work was another matter entirely.

"I'll see what I can do," Ian promised.

The agent thanked him and said he would call again in the morning to see what the response of the Kirk Session had been.

Ian sighed and set his mobile back on its base to recharge. Time to face off with the church ladies then.

Before he could move, his mobile rang again.

This time, it was his overseer, a man for whom he shared a great mutual respect and much camaraderie.

"Ian, I'm calling to ask you to speak at the Argyle Ministerial Association's Retreat for Pastors this summer."

Ian smiled broadly and felt his spirits lift. It was a great honor to be asked to speak before your peers, and the invitation confirmed what he'd always felt from his overseer – that the man valued and appreciated him – a much more satisfying affirmation than the fact that the church ladies of St. Conan's thought he was "cute".

He accepted his overseer's invitation without reservation, and his supervisor promised to email him the specifics about the time, date, and location of the convocation as well as the theme and scriptures that had been selected for the retreat.

When he returned to the room where the ladies were quilting, he found the caramel shortbread gone. The topic of conversation had changed from Chelsea's prospects for the future to the manure Margaret Ainsworth's neighbor had spread on the field adjacent to her house and the resulting stench. He considered reintroducing the question of whom Chelsea Downey should marry, but decided against it in the end. He didn't want to offend Edith, and of course, he was sure nothing would come of the conversation anyway.

Chapter 7

Wednesday dawned as fair as a bonnie lassie. When Ian awakened to sunshine, he decided to take the insurance agent's recommendation to heart and spend a bit of time in the garden. He'd start by trimming the bushes and weeding the areas along the steps and walkways where the grass and thistles were overtaking the path.

He was caught up on his paperwork and had not only finished phoning each member of the Kirk Session, he'd notified the insurance company that the dreaded deductible could be raised to 10,000 pounds to help defray the amount that was in arrears as well as next years premiums.

He put on his heaviest pair of protective gloves and gingerly grasped the base of a thistle. The thorns were already well developed despite the plant's young age, and he could feel the points pricking through the gloves the second he started to apply pressure and tug.

A few seconds later, a long, intricate root system emerged from the ground, spraying soil over his boots and the cobblestone walkway. One down, dozens to go. It appeared that the thistle was a symbol of Scotland's tenacity for good reason.

The worst thing was the way the tendrils insinuated themselves in and around the stone, crumbling and heaving and buckling everything in their path.

He could feel his neck shining with the sheen of perspiration, the sun beating down on his back, and fine particles of dirt clinging to his face. He had pulled no more than a dozen of the little buggers. There were hundreds to go.

He was wishing he had reason to take a break when he heard a voice. "Ian?"

He straightened and simultaneously rose from his crouched position and turned to see who it was. "Emily?"

"I hope you don't mind me dropping by again."

She smiled, at the same time looking relaxed yet prim in her pink and lavender plaid skirt and matching scarf, her cheeks a rosy hue, he assumed from the sunshine and the nippy spring air.

"No, no. Of course not," he stammered.

"I was in Oban doing a presentation for the ferry company – they're trying to update and enhance their image after the recent fiasco with the collision."

"That's right. A man was killed."

"And everyone on board stranded for hours, many with scrapes and bruises."

"It must have been horrifying."

"It was."

"I'm sure that leaves you with a challenging task."

"It's what I'm trained to do. Put a positive spin on things. Make the worst scenario seem no cause for concern."

"It went well then?"

"I have a stack of press releases and a new ad campaign ready to go as soon as I get back to Glasgow."

"Congratulations then."

"Let's wait on that until we see if it works. Everything always looks good on paper – that doesn't mean things will work out the way we hope they will in reality."

He nodded, suddenly, inexplicably aware that she was talking about a picture much bigger than ferries running into fishing boats.

"You're right," she said, with the same intent gaze he'd come to expect from her. "I don't love Benjamin. He's wonderful – he really is. He's everything I want in a husband. He'll make a wonderful father one day. I admire him greatly, and respect him. I even like him. I love everything about him, but I don't love him."

Ian sighed and rocked back on his heels. "You said that he loves you. Is that really the case, or is this a marriage of convenience for both of you?"

She looked so vulnerable, so shattered, so scared.

"No. I believe he truly loves me with all his heart and soul and mind. I think that's what terrifies me the most. If we were of like mind, it wouldn't matter, would it?"

"As in honor among thieves?"

"You're right. This is absolutely unfair to Benjamin. I've mislead him and withheld the best parts of myself from him." She started to weep and went to the stone wall overlooking the loch.

He went to her side and stood with her, looking out at waters so still, calm, and unruffled that a perfect reflection of everything hovering over them could be seen in the glassy surface.

"Don't give up quite yet," Ian said, wondering which was worse, a sister who loved and was determined to marry an absolute deadbeat, or a sister who couldn't quite let herself love a man who sounded as though he was an ideal candidate for a husband. "Let's talk, the three of us, and see what comes out of it. Will you do that for me?"

"Yes." She leaned down, found a flat pebble, and skipped it over the surface of the loch. She turned and looked at him then, her longing deep and palpable.

He knew he needed to be careful not to lead her on, but he wanted to help. What he could say that would soothe her without crossing that line? "You know as well as I do that half of the problem is realizing there is a problem."

"You can't fix a problem until you've identified what the problem is," she repeated. "I learned that in my first Public Relations class."

"Then your task is clear. Try to make things right."

"But how?"

"Let me think on it a bit. I'm going to pray that Benjamin will be able to accompany you on Saturday."

Her face was full of uncertainty. She was used to being in control.

"Trust me," he said.

"I do."

"Between now and then, I want you to make a list of all the things you love about Benjamin and all the things you love about yourself and your life."

"Okay," she said. "I can do that."

"And put as positive a spin on things as you like."

"Okay. I will." Her face lit up and she smiled.

"And I want you to prepare two statements – the official company position – the one that goes out to the public."

"Yes."

"And another, a 'for your eyes only' version of events. No one will see it but you, so I want you to be totally honest – your true feelings, your innermost thoughts and deepest fears. Can you do that?"

"Yes." Her eyes were shining. She actually looked excited.

"Go then. Get started now while it's clear in your mind what you need to do."

"I will." She looked up, and he watched as the long curve of her neck arched back. Maybe she was invoking help from above, perhaps she was counting her lucky stars. He didn't venture a guess. And then she said, "Pastor Ian, isn't that where the copper rabbit drain spout used to be?"

She pointed to the expanse of roof just to the left of the flying buttresses. "Has he been taken down for repairs?"

"No." Ian looked up, and a siren started clanging in his head. "Where on earth?" He looked around to reassess their whereabouts. They were exactly where he'd thought they were. The rabbit was gone.

He rushed to the spot directly beneath the drain spout and combed the tall grasses. Had a bracket rusted, allowing the precious rabbit to fall? Nothing. His eyes flew from one turret to another. When was the last time he'd looked up? Was anything else missing? How could this be? To quote the insurance agent, who would steal from a church?

"Let's go inside." In his rush, he very nearly tripped over the same clump of thistles and grasses he'd been trying to unearth. He hadn't checked the donation box since Monday morning, and hadn't emptied it then. How long had it been? A week? A fortnight was probably more like it. It wasn't high tourist season, but one never knew when someone with a generous gift might stumble by. He sped through the cloistered abbey with Emily in hot pursuit. *Gone.* He twirled around on the smooth stone flooring so fast that it made his head spin. The baptismal font – gone. How could he not have noticed? It had been there on Monday, that was certain. Where had he been since then that he hadn't noticed something so blatantly wrong?

He'd worked from his kitchen table most of Tuesday, gone to visit some elderly shut-ins, taken them communion, done some errands in Inveraray, picked up a few groceries. This morning, he'd gone directly to the gardens.

How could this have happened? Why had this happened? So much for a hedge of protection surrounding the kirk. They'd been stripped bare of their most valuable assets.

Thistle Down

Chapter 8

For reasons Ian had never really identified or even given much thought, the constable had never been one of his favorite people. But the man was certainly being helpful today, and he was grateful for that.

Ian looked across the constable's desk, then over his shoulder to make sure the door to the man's office was shut tightly. He really wasn't fond of the notion that news of St. Conan's robbery be broadcast all over Argyle. "Would it help if we were to install a surveillance camera?"

"Only an idiot would return to the scene of the crime. These kinds of petty thieves go in, take what they want, and move on to the next heist."

In Ian's opinion, stealing easily-identifiable, traceable items like the copper rabbit and one-of-a-kind baptismal font from St. Conan's was precisely something only an idiot would do, but he didn't express his thoughts out loud.

"Is there anything else we can do to enhance our security? I want to avoid any kind of repeat occurrence. My fear is that now that they know that the place is wide open and unguarded much of the time, we're an easy target for return visits. Robert the Bruce's bone, our lovely stained glass – there are all kinds of unique architectural artifacts still ripe for the taking."

"You could keep the kirk locked. I know it goes against the grain, but many places are starting to do it."

"Locking the doors wouldn't have saved the copper rabbit."

"No, but it would protect Bruce's bones. The wife and I took a trip to Scandinavia last year and didn't get inside a single church. Locked up tight, every last one of them. And Danes and Norwegians are reputedly some of the most honest folks on earth. Our tour guide said it was due to high incidences of both thievery and vandalism."

Vandalism? He'd never even considered it to be a risk. "Could this have been some sort of childish prank then? Teenagers?"

"I doubt that. And you shouldnae necessarily equate vandalism with harmless teens. I've a cousin in America who lives in an area where there have been several churches burned to the ground. In this day and age, vandals can be far more dangerous than the pranksters of my era. Perhaps it's issues with the church, the pastor, or with Christianity in general, but there are those among us who would do anything to see the church and its traditions destroyed."

A chilling thought, and one he hated to even think about. "But if it was teenagers, doing it just to prove it could be done, the artifacts might still be returned, correct?"

"Sometimes part of the thrill is returning the items without getting caught. I wouldn't hold my breath if I were you."

"I dread telling the elders what has happened. It's been a challenging winter already, what with both giving and attendance down because of the bad weather."

"We can try to keep it quiet for a few days." The man wiped his mouth on the back of his hand. "You know how people are. Whoever was with you when you noticed the rabbit was gone must be pretty discreet, because normally, news like this would be all over Lochawe before we put our heads to the pillow."

Ian sighed. Emily was to be commended then. As he did on many an occasion, he wondered why it was that he was expected to keep everything confidential, while the rest of the town had free license to gossip about anything and everything that went on.

"The problem is, if it was teenagers, it would be to your benefit for them to find out that you know as soon as possible so they can get their jollies, feel superior, and return the things they pilfered."

"I suppose you're right. Once they've had their fun..." Ian slipped his hands into his pockets. "And if it wasn't a prank – is there any hope of recovering the things that were stolen?"

"I won't lie to a man of the cloth. It's rare."

"Is there anything else I can do – we can do?"

"If you're serious aboot keeping a closer eye on the place, another option would be to have volunteers manning the church whenever you can't be there personally. Call them tour guides or greeters or attendants, or whatever you like. The kirk could still be open to tourists and worshippers every day without sacrificing the safety of the historical artifacts you still have."

That was putting it bluntly. "I can barely round up enough

people to act as ushers, communion assistants and greeters on Sunday mornings." Thank goodness they had a faithful organist who was present and in good form every Sunday. Filling the other positions was hit and miss at best.

"Just a thought. I'm not sure how much you're around, or if you have a secretary."

"I've a part time assistant who works only a few hours a week. When I'm not visiting the elderly or infirmed, I'm usually working at my house. It's considerably warmer at the manse than it is in my office at the church."

"If you trimmed away some of the underbrush surrounding your cottage, you'd have a clear vision of what's going on in the churchyard."

"And sacrifice what little privacy I have."

"We can try to keep an eye open for suspicious persons or activities going on at the church, but it's pretty much a moot point as long as you have tourists coming and going all day long."

"I understand what you're saying, but being a sanctuary for travelers and townspeople alike has been an important part of our ministry for years. People come from every county in Scotland and nearly every country in the world to visit St. Conan's. It would be a shame to put an end to that."

"A chain with a big padlock across the gate would go a long way towards discouraging random visitors."

"That would be a sad day indeed."

The constable glanced over his shoulder and looked about the room like he feared the walls had ears. "When you originally informed me that the items were missing, my first thought was, 'Who would steal from a church?'"

"And what answer have you come up with, then?"

"We've talked about someone who could be so stupid, someone who's out to make a statement, and someone who's getting their kicks as possibilities, but there's one other personality profile that we've failed to consider."

"Yes?"

"Someone who would steal from a church could well be someone who is morally bankrupt, someone who has no conscience."

Ian felt a chill wash over him. "I hate to think that someone of that description would have set their sights on an out-of-the-way place like St. Conan's."

"As do I, laddie. But it would heed you to entertain the possibility, because if - heaven forbid I'm right, that person could also be a very real danger to you or anyone else who dared stand in his way."

This gave Ian definite pause for thought. "I will take heed."

"Best watch your back until we've conducted our investigation."

What about the church ladies? Who would look out for them? Ian didn't want to alarm them unduly, but shouldn't they be told to watch their steps until the man was apprehended, if ever?

"I'll be in touch," the constable promised. "Let me know what you decide to do aboot the surveillance camera and we'll do what we can in the meantime."

Chapter 9

Saturday dawned clear and bright. The weather had finally taken a turn for the better and the spring-like temperatures they'd all been wishing for were finally upon them. Ian was so happy that he felt like singing along with the birds in the rhododendrons outside his door.

If he hadn't had a session scheduled with Emily and Benjamin for the afternoon, he'd have dusted the cobwebs off his bicycle and ridden out into the country. He loved the smells of springtime – the loamy earth unthawing and turning to mud, plants shooting up from the soil, the earth waking up.

But duty called.

He was pleasantly surprised when Emily Downey walked in the door with Benjamin in tow.

"Ian - I mean Pastor Ian - this is Benjamin." Her voice was shy and hesitant.

Benjamin reached out and clasped his hand confidently. "It's nice to finally meet you. Emily's whole family raves about you."

Ian noticed that Emily was blushing, but she didn't say anything.

"Sorry again that I missed our first session."

"No need," Ian said. "It worked out rather nicely now that you mention it. Emily and I had a chance to get acquainted."

"So she tells me." He smiled broadly and Ian sensed only sincerity from him.

"I've never been to Loch Awe or St. Conan's, and I must say, I'm impressed. It's a lovely trip up from Glasgow."

"It's a beautiful kirk. I feel privileged to have been given this call."

"That's an interesting way to put it," Benjamin said, looking genuinely fascinated with what Ian was saying. "I feel the same way about medicine. It's my job, the profession I've chosen, and yet it's so much more than that."

"Serving people always is," Ian said.

"As is healing," Benjamin said. "God's work, our hands."

"Exactly."

They spent the next fifteen or twenty minutes getting to know each other, comparing notes, sharing the joys and privileges of their callings as well as the occasional frustrations, even an amusing anecdote or two. Emily listened intently, looking from one to the other, following the conversation with her intelligent brown eyes, mirroring all the appropriate emotions and responses.

Perhaps it was because Benjamin's personality was such a welcome departure from Greg's insolence, maybe it was simply that they had so much in common, but before Ian realized it, an hour had flown by and Emily hadn't said more than a word or two.

He felt terrible when he realized what he'd done – and not done. He tried to correct his faux pas. "Emily, how do you feel about being a doctor's wife?"

She cleared her throat and smiled at Benjamin. "Well, as you know, I've already gotten a pretty good taste of what it's like to have to contend with long hours, no days off, and emergency calls. But I've been on my own for over a decade, so I'm used to it and more. I know how to take care of myself. And I'm very proud of Benjamin's..." She hesitated. "Calling."

Fair enough, except that her response sounded like a prepared statement for a press release. But then, that was what he'd urged her to do. At least, that had been part of her assignment.

Benjamin squeezed her hand and smiled at her. "Emily has a great gift for what she does, too. I've gone to her for guidance on how to handle a cantankerous patient or co-worker more times than I can count. She gives very sound advice."

"So tell me some of the things that the two of you enjoy doing together," Ian said, feeling more relaxed and at ease than he had in weeks.

"We enjoy playing Scrabble," Benjamin said.

"Yes," Emily said. "Except for the fact that Benjamin has a tendency to gloat when he wins."

"Emily is also an excellent golfer."

"And when I win at golf, I'm afraid I do a somewhat irritating victory dance on the 18th green."

"Have you ever played Carnoustie?" Ian asked him, her – both of them.

"I have," Benjamin answered. "Don't you love the way the burn seems to reach up and grab your ball just when you think you've hit a good shot?"

"And the way the greens slope down to the ocean, and the breezes off the water."

"I've not played there, yet," Emily said quietly. "I'd love to, one day."

Benjamin's face lit up. "I took off my shoes and socks and rolled up my pants and waded into the water to try to hit my ball on the 18th hole a la Van de Beld."

They spent the next ten minutes discussing the courses they'd played, and the fact that Ian had worked as a golf pro between graduating from college and beginning his training at St. Andrew's Theological Seminary.

Again, Emily sat quietly by while the two of them went on about this course and that.

"Um, looking at the results of your inventory," Ian said, realizing once more that they had gotten off track. "It appears that you're very well-matched. Your results indicate that you're a Vitalized Couple, which means that your relationship is harmonious in all areas, with a strong likelihood of success."

"That's wonderful," Benjamin said. "Isn't it, dear?"

"Yes. Yes. Of course it is."

Ian smiled. "In the different categories of the questionnaire – Communication, Conflict Resolution, Financial Management, Leisure Activities, Friends and Family Acceptance, Marital Expectations, Parental Roles, Sexual Compatibility, Personality Types – which do each of you see as your strongest asset, and conversely, your weakest, or the area in which you will likely need to experience growth?"

Ian knew he was being childish, but he prayed that neither of them said Sexual Compatibility. First, there was the matter of Emily's erratic behavior towards him, and now that he'd established a friendly rapport with her fiancé, he suspected it would be awkward having a clinical discussion about something so personal as sex. Except of course, that Benjamin was a doctor, probably even trained in these matters.

Emily spoke first. "I think our strongest would be Friends and Family Acceptance. Everyone loves Benjamin." For a second, her eyes bored daggers though Ian's. *Except me.* "And for our weakest, I'd have to say Conflict Resolution."

"May I ask why?" Ian asked.

"It's hard to get mad at someone who's perfect. And so well liked."

"Okay," Ian said. *A surprising answer for an expert at public relations.* "What about you, Benjamin? Would you agree?"

Benjamin looked a little mystified, but he answered, "From my perspective, I feel that Communication would be our strong suit, and our improvement-needed category would have to be Leisure Activities – basically, because we have so little time for anything besides work."

"Emily, do you think Benjamin is a good communicator?"

"The best," she said dully. "I can't fault him for anything."

"Benjamin, do you think Emily is good at conflict resolution?"

"I think she's excellent at it when she's on the outside looking in. When she's the one embroiled in the conflict, I get a sense that it's harder for her."

"In what way?" This from Emily.

"Well, all I meant is that it's a little difficult to engage you at times."

"Oh?"

"We've discussed the fact that you can come across as being a little aloof."

"That's right. We have. Because you're such an excellent communicator."

"I know it's not intentional, dear."

"Oh do you?" Emily whipped around to glare at Ian before turning back to Benjamin.

"Of course, I do."

"Well, well, maybe you should think again then, sweetheart. Because... well, I am holding back, and I'm doing it on purpose."

Benjamin looked as though he was absolutely shocked. "But, Emily-"

"It's true, Benjamin. You're too perfect. And I just can't stay in this plastic relationship any longer!"

"What are you saying?" Benjamin seemed not to be too worried. He did look concerned for Emily, although his basic confidence seemed unruffled.

"That I can't marry you. You're perfect on paper, but-"

"But what? We've discussed all of this. Passion, acting silly, puppy love aren't part of my personality. Yours either. But that's okay. Passion fades over time anyway. What we have is much wiser, richer, more meaningful than-"

"I've changed my mind," she said. "I love everything about you, but I don't... I don't want to..."

What happened next certainly had to be classified as a miracle, certainly no less beautiful, no less significant than Jesus turning water into wine or making the blind to see.

Benjamin lost it. "So this is the way you tell me you're breaking up with me?" He sounded angry. He was angry.

"What would you prefer? That I do it over perfectly prepared hors d'euvres and a forty pound bottle of wine at a five star restaurant?"

"No. Yes. I don't know."

Emily looked half terrified, half jubilant. "Neither do I. I don't know what I want."

"Yes you do," Benjamin snapped. "You want it all. You're a high achiever, alpha, perfectionist just like I am, and unless you have it all, you're never going to be happy."

"You're absolutely right." Now she looked angry. "You always are. You're so sickeningly right that it's nauseating."

"Then why is my stomach tied in knots? And why does my head feel like it's going to explode? And why is my heart pounding like I've just run a marathon?"

Ian had this one. "Because you're afraid you're going to lose her."

"I hate that she makes me feel this way. Out of control. Discombobulated. Crazed."

Ian smiled. "Like a man in love. Passionately and completely in love."

Benjamin hadn't moved, but he was sweating, and his hair was ruffled, and his eyes were wild. "I love you so very much, Emily. I'd be lost without you. Please say you'll marry me."

"Do you mean it?" Emily's eyes were tremulous with wonder, her eyelashes laden with big, heavy tears.

"I wouldn't say it if I didn't."

"Benjamin has told you what he's feeling, Emily. Tell him what you feel. Not what you think, what you feel right at this moment."

"I feel it." She started to tremble. "I'm not sure what, but I think I feel passion." She said the word shakily, like she'd tasted some sort of extremely exotic food for the very first time. "At least that's what I think it is. I've never... I mean, this is a new experience for me."

"Oh, sweetheart."

Suddenly, it was as though the pages of a romance novel had come to life. Benjamin reached for her, and Emily crushed herself against his chest, and they were kissing and crying and clutching and... That's when Ian left the room, and closed the door behind him.

Chapter 10

"Pastor Ian?"

Ian looked up from his sermon notes to see a thatch of curly red hair and a smile fit to make the heavens sing framed in the stone archway that led to his office. "Emily. How nice of you to stop back. Is Benjamin here?"

"One of his patients took a turn for the worse and he had to rush back to Glasgow."

"I'm sorry."

"No. It's fine. I wanted to stay the weekend so Mom and I could get started on wedding plans. We visited a florist this afternoon and spoke to a caterer about food for the reception."

"I'm very happy for you, Emily."

"Thank you, Ian. And thank you, too, for everything – I mean, I really appreciate all that you did to help Benjamin and me work through our problems."

"I wish the two of you much happiness."

Emily smiled and turned to go. "Oh. I forgot to ask about the missing items. Any ideas about where they disappeared to?"

"It definitely appears to have been a theft. I made some inquiries and no one on the Kirk Session had removed any of the items for repairs or refurbishing."

"Who would do such a thing?"

"I have no idea. Thank you for keeping it quiet until I'd had a chance to notify the authorities. It will be up to the session to decide when and how to inform the rest of the congregation."

"No sense marring their Easter with the news."

"My thought exactly. We've better things to dwell on as we approach Holy Week." Ian stood and walked with Emily.

"Still, I hope they catch the man and that the items gone missing will be returned."

"The constable said we're not to hold out much hope."

"It's kind of funny when you think about it. Telling a church not to have hope." Emily smiled.

"God knows who took the things and where every last item is at this precise moment. The constable may be the one who's in for a surprise before all is said and done."

"We do believe in a God of miracles."

"Yes, we do."

Emily's face was shining with a combination of what he assumed was contentment – perhaps joy. Funny, he had never noticed it before now. Well, then, she was living proof of God's grace, wasn't she? "And a God who is known to work in mysterious ways."

Chapter 11

The first thing Ian noticed when he walked into the sanctuary at St. Conan's the next morning was that everyone was looking at him differently. Ladies were batting their eyes and fluttering their eyelashes and one even winked at him. What had changed, he wasn't quite sure, but it was almost like they were looking at him – for the first time – as not just a pastor, but a man.

Was his zipper down? Did he have a cowlick in his hair? He knew it wasn't lipstick on his collar or spinach in his teeth because he hadn't had any in years. Sad to say.

No one had said anything about the baptismal font being gone and he didn't intend to mention it unless they asked. It was sometimes stored in the rear of the kirk to make more room for the children or the choir when they rose to sing. Or perhaps they thought it was temporarily gone for refurbishing or cleaning. Whatever the case, its absence didn't appear to be alarming anyone and that was fine with him. It certainly didn't account for the strange behavior of the people gathered around him.

He was saying hello to Shirley Wilson when one of the men punched him in the arm and grinned devilishly. What was up with that?

He looked around as he walked toward the pulpit, mystified to say the least. And then he saw Margaret Ainsworth. There was something about her... the way she stopped talking the second he started to approach her, the slightly apologetic look in her eyes as he grew nearer, the silent look she gave to the people she'd been speaking to...

"Hello, Margaret."

"Why Pastor Ian," she said, glancing at the others as if to say, *Watch me – I'll show you how it's done.* "We've just been talking and wondering if you have plans for Easter dinner next week."

Where was this going? In all the years he'd been at St. Conan's, he'd never been invited to Easter dinner before.

"Haven't you always said that it's too far to drive the distance to your mother's house by the time you finish services?" Edith Downey asked.

"Well, yes, but there's the church breakfast. I've never gone hungry." The ladies of the church always served breakfast between the sunrise service and regular worship. The platter of leftovers they sent home with him was enough to feed him for several days.

"It must be lonely for you, Pastor, alone at the manse, day after day, week after week, month after-"

"I'm quite used to the solitude, actually, and I'm never far from people, living right next to the church, now am I?" To be honest, he was always so exhausted after the rigors of the Holy Week schedule that he relished the time alone.

"Being around all of us, and people in general, is no substitute for having someone special in your life though, is it now?"

A trap. "I suppose not. But-"

"But you're in your thirties now, aren't you? Certainly you want children one day, don't you? A family of your own?"

"Of course I do."

"Well, then, time's a wastin'."

"We just thought you'd like to meet more young people your own age," another of the ladies said. "Instead of spending so much time with us older ladies."

It seemed ironic to him that if more members of the younger generation came to church with any regularity, he'd know plenty of them by now. When he'd first come to St. Conan's, he'd hoped having a young pastor would draw in young people, but it hadn't happened, at least not yet.

"The Bible study I've got scheduled for next month is geared towards young couples. I've even arranged for child care during the study. I hope-"

"But it's singles you need to be meeting, Pastor Ian. Your social life is not going to be enhanced by studying the Scriptures with a bunch of couples."

"Really, ladies – I appreciate your concern, but my social life is in God's hands along with the rest of my daily comings and goings, and I'm happy to leave it there."

Margaret smiled smugly. "But dear, you said it yourself in last week's sermon – God helps those who help themselves."

He didn't recall ever saying that phrase in any sermon he had ever given, but whatever.

A friend of Margaret's said, "Won't Chelsea and Emily be at your family's Easter celebration, Margaret?"

"Why, yes. They will be. I hadn't thought of that. And how perfect, since Pastor Ian already knows them."

"So there would be plenty to talk about," Edith chimed in shamelessly.

"And he'd feel right at home."

"But-"

"And I'm sure Chelsea would appreciate the company since Greg's not coming," Edith said.

So that was what this was all about. He should have seen it coming.

"Ladies, I know you're concerned about Chelsea-" He was just about to set the record straight when the bells started ringing and the acolytes started up the isle. He was supposed to be in the rear of the church, ready to process with the palm branches.

He looked from one hopeful face to the next, at a loss as to how to get them to understand the utter preposterousness of their scheme. Did they really think that a minister could go from counseling a betrothed couple to stealing the bride for himself? If he even wanted to, which of course, he didn't. It was ridiculous. And now, flushed and distracted and discombobulated, they wanted him to preach a sermon?

He had a mind to quickly change the Scripture lesson to I Peter 4:15 – *But let none of you suffer as a murderer. Or a thief, or an evildoer, or as a busybody in other men's matters.*

Of course, there were some who would say that was exactly what he was doing each and every time Emily and Benjamin or Chelsea and Greg walked into his office for counseling.

He sighed and turned to follow the acolyte the remaining few steps to the front of the kirk, praying for divine wisdom once again.

Chapter 12

Ian was waiting at his desk when Greg and Chelsea entered his office later that afternoon. This week, he'd actually been relieved when the couple hadn't shown up for worship, given the church ladies' antics.

Greg looked marginally less hostile than he had the week before. Chelsea seemed to be wound even more tightly than she had been at their previous meetings. One had to wonder what Greg had said to her on their way to the kirk.

Ian's immediate concern had been that Greg wouldn't come to the next counseling session. Now, he realized his error. Greg would be at each and every session. There was no way Greg would allow Chelsea to come by herself or risk her having a conversation of which he wasn't in control.

"So, how many of these things do we have to come to?" Greg asked.

Ian resisted the urge to roll his eyes. *Really, was that the best Greg could do? To act like a five year old to get his way?* "Four."

"I thought it was just three," Chelsea said.

"I think we'll find plenty to talk about to fill today's session and two more."

"The sooner we get started, the sooner we can get out of here," Greg pointed out.

Okay. There was definite hostility in the air. Since Ian hadn't seen or spoken to either of them all week, he had to assume that what had changed was something between the two of them. Had they been fighting about what they would share while at counseling? Arguing about the wedding? Disagreeing about where they would live once they'd tied the knot?

It was time to change his strategy. At the rate this session was going, it could be their last. It was time to get down to business. He could live with a redeemed Greg and Chelsea. He could live with Greg and Chelsea going their separate ways. But he could not stand the thought of marrying this couple with so many issues between them still unresolved.

"We're going to talk about your wedding vows today."

"I thought I was supposed to write a song."

"We can save it for the end."

"I want to sing it now."

Ian looked at Chelsea, who sat frozen in her chair.

"Fine. You go ahead, Greg."

Greg punched a button on his MP3 player and a rap beat started playing. "My baby brings me beer. Empty can? Hey – never fear, cuz my baby, Chelsea's, here. Hey babe, I need a beer, served with just a smile, some cheer, now don't let me hear you jeer, you bunch of weir-dos, cuz my Chell is great at refilling beers."

"That's what you wrote about me? That's all you think I'm good for?" Chelsea burst into tears.

Greg smiled and didn't even attempt to comfort her. *The jerk.*

"Greg, it sounds to me like you only like Chelsea when she does want you want her to. And that if she were to stand up for herself and do what she thinks is right, that you wouldn't like her any more."

"That's not fair." Chelsea swiped at her tears and rose to Greg's defense.

Greg's defense?

"It's just a song. He's just joking. All his songs are like tongue in cheek. They're a parody."

Greg laughed. "Naw, that's pretty much what I think of her."

"You," Ian said. "She's here in the room. If you're going to say it, say it to her. If you're going to slam the woman you supposedly love, then be a man, look her in the eyes and say it to her face."

"But-" Chelsea squeaked.

"Let Greg speak," Ian said.

"But-"

"No. It's fine, Babe. I do like you because you're so nice to me. Is that a crime?"

"Chelsea is a very smart, very capable, very talented woman, Greg. You don't think this song is demeaning to all that she is and all that she's accomplished?"

Chelsea visibly flared. "Greg is very talented, too. And he's probably smarter than I am in a lot of ways."

Right. He has a real knack for making women feel worthless.

Greg clearly excelled at that.

Chelsea was still sniffling, and why she was mad at Ian and not Greg, Ian couldn't begin to fathom.

Now they were both glaring at him.

"So – let's talk about your marriage vows."

"What if I don't want to?" Greg said.

Ian ignored him. "Greg, I noticed on the questionnaire that you filled out that you neglected to respond to the sections about whether or not you have children from any previous relationships."

Greg looked at him, his eyes full of insolence and belligerence, and a few other assorted emotions that a pastor rarely sees. Because for better or worse, most people were on their best behavior when they were in the presence of the pastor. Most people tried to hide their worst traits, not only when they were at church, but when they were trying to impress their future spouse. Unless this was Greg's good side.

"Greg?"

"You've been talking to Emily, haven't you?" Chelsea turned on him like a rabid dog. "She's been spreading lies about Greg since day one. She's just jealous! She didn't even have a boyfriend until a few months ago, and she couldn't stand the fact that Greg and I are so happy, and that I had someone to love and she didn't."

Greg didn't say a word, but his eyes were not only staking their claim, they were taunting Ian with victory.

Go ahead and try to split us up, Greg was saying, as loud and clear as a person could, non-verbally. *Give it your best shot, dude. Makes no difference to me. Cause I know – you know – you're gonna fail.*

"Chelsea, we've established the fact that you're going to be a great lawyer. You're very adept at defending your cause. But I'd like to hear what Greg has to say," Ian said.

"But-"

"Hey." Greg cut her off. "It's cool, Babe. Like I said, one of the major reasons I like being with you is because you do nice stuff for me like getting me more beer when I don't want to get up. Is that a crime?"

"Of course not, sweetheart. I love waiting on you. I'm just sorry I'm not home more often. I'd love it if I could take care of you 24 by 7." Chelsea leaned over and kissed Greg's nose.

For a moment, Ian thought he might be ill. How could a man be so good looking on the outside yet so foul on the inside? He took a deep breath. "Okay. Moving on to your vows. Wilt thou have this woman to be thy wedded wife, to live together after God's ordinance in the holy estate of matrimony? Wilt thou love her?"

"Of course he will," Chelsea snapped. "Would he have asked me to marry him if he didn't love me?"

Greg just leered at him.

"Wilt thou comfort her?"

"Greg is the best snuggler in the world." Chelsea reached down and tried to twine her fingers through Greg's. He kept his fists clenched for a moment, then reluctantly let her pry apart his fingers.

"Wilt thou honor and keep her in sickness and in health?"

"Only if she can still walk to the refrigerator and get me more beer."

"Anything else?" Ian asked facetiously.

"Well, you know, she'd have to be able to do it."

Chelsea's face crinkled up like she was going to laugh, but when Greg didn't, she didn't.

"Wilt thou forsake all others, and keep thee only unto her, so long as ye both shall live?"

"What about for richer or poorer? Why did you skip that part? 'Cause we've been poor ever since we met, and when Chelsea starts raking in the big bucks the guys and I are going to buy a new motor home and catch the first ferry for the mainland."

Greg wasn't stupid. He was just confident that Chelsea was so firmly under his control that she wouldn't leave him even if he told her the truth and flaunted it right in her face. She was so afraid of losing him that she would never call him on his oafish behavior. And he knew it.

"Greg, you've evaded my questions about children, and now you've refused to promise that you'll be faithful to Chelsea. How about the truth? Do you have any intention of pledging yourself to Chelsea or do you intend to keep sleeping with every woman who will have you?"

Now Greg laughed. But Chelsea didn't. She blinked and looked at Greg, then at Ian. "Do you really think Greg would...?"

"Greg?"

"Hey – they change these stupid vows all the time anyway. That whole shtick about what God has joined together, let no man put asunder isn't worth the paper it's written on any more. More people get divorced these days than stay married. And no normal woman in today's day and age would pledge to obey her husband, so what did they do? They took out that part. Well, no respecting man I know would ever promise to never sleep with another woman for the rest of his life, so you know what we all think? You should take it out. If the women won't obey us, then we won't be made to be faithful to them."

Ian just looked him. Chelsea didn't utter a peep.

"What?" Greg scratched himself. "Everybody knows it's physiologically impossible anyway. Men are made to be hound dogs."

"Men are made in God's image, and with His help, they are perfectly capable of remaining faithful to one woman."

"So is what they all say true?" Chelsea's voice squeaked out of her mouth like a balloon loosing its air, her gusto gone. "Is Charlie your baby?"

"His mother is a lying slut. That's what everybody knows."

"But did you sleep with her?"

Greg just grinned. "You know the deal, babe. A witness isn't allowed to incriminate himself. It's the law." And then he laughed like it was the funniest thing in the world.

"What about the rest then?" Chelsea had tears running down her face. "Is the little girl who belongs to that tramp who comes to hear the band play all the time your daughter?"

Greg shrugged.

"Oh my God." Chelsea moaned. "All my friends have been trying to tell me for months, and I wouldn't... I believed you."

Greg still looked unfazed, even a little cocky. The man simply didn't believe Chelsea would leave him. And maybe she wouldn't.

Ian turned to her. "I'm sorry, Chelsea." He wanted to say more, to tell her that she was a wonderful woman who deserved to be honored and cherished and admired, that she would be better off alone than with a man who treated her with such blatant disregard, that she should hold out for someone who loved her, for heaven's sake.

Chelsea and Greg were glaring at each other now, she, like, *How could you?* And he, like, *What's with you?*

Ian sighed. Maybe if he had more experience... He sometimes wondered if his critics were right. Maybe he had no business dispensing advice on relationships when he was such a novice himself.

Greg stood. "Let's get out of here, Babe. We don't need this."

Please God. Ian prayed. *Do not leave with him.* He held his breath, not daring to look at Chelsea, but at the same time, wanting to hold his hand out to her, or worse – to grab her and forcibly keep her there. He didn't want to say the wrong thing, to make things worse than they already were. He didn't know what to do. So he kept on praying.

And then Chelsea stood. Ian's heart leaped in his chest. He jumped to his feet and took a step towards the door. It wasn't his place to block the door or forbid her to leave, but oh, how he wanted to.

"Greg, I want to thank you for being honest with me and with Chelsea." He wanted to make it clear - crystal clear - that he did not believe Greg was joshing, teasing or being funny.

He looked at Chelsea. *Come to me, sweetheart. You can find sanctuary here. I can help you.* He prayed silently. It was up to her now. Up to her as to whether or not she could live with the truth of who Greg was and what kind of marriage they would have.

Chelsea reached out her fingers and clasped Greg's outstretched hand. And followed him out the door.

Chapter 13

Ian knew that Easter Sunday was about Jesus dying on the cross and rising again, but after a long hard winter and a slow start to spring, he couldn't help but associate the season with baby lambs, jonquils, Cadbury Cream Eggs and colorful Easter bonnets as well.

Every pew was full as he looked out over the sanctuary at St. Conan's. Sunshine streamed through the stained glass windows and the tensions of the proceeding week seemed to evaporate with every word that he spoke, every song of jubilation that was sung. It was a glorious day, one of the absolute highlights of the entire year for a pastor, and hopefully, his congregants as well.

"We have two images to think about today. First, the prickly thorns and piercing nails that Christ endured while suffering the trials of his crucifixion. Being one with Christ means that like him, we must, at times, bear the stinging ache of despair. Feeling pain means that we're alive. Jesus knows what it's like to be tempted, to be disappointed and hurt. He knows what it's like to experience pain and rejection, to ache with despair and grief.

"By contrast, we see comforting images in the Easter story as well – the Spirit of God of descending like a dove from the heavens, tender, loving arms lifting Jesus' body from the cross, soft cloths wrapped around his body, precious spices poured out to anoint his wounds. To need, to love and be loved, and to feel tenderness, also means that we're human. We are made in Jesus' image. There is joy in being cared for. Softly and tenderly, Jesus calls us to follow him through pain and sorrow, even through the valley of the shadow of death.

"But there is more to this story. Jesus suffered and died a painful, prickly death, then rose to experience new life. Throughout the scriptures, we see the image of sunshine and joy after rain, the rainbow after the storm, thorny stems producing rosebuds, the pain of childbirth leading to joy. Jesus died so that we might have life, and have it more abundantly. There was joy when the women at the tomb discovered that Jesus had risen. They had witnessed a terrible ordeal, but they found joy in the morning.

"Scotland's dear thistles are one more example of this priceless analogy. Prickly, hurtful thorns, and soft, downy seeds drifting in the wind, spreading the message that life goes on even when our days are riddled with pain and hardship."

By the time he finished his sermon, served communion and greeted the dozens of extra visitors who had attended the service, he was exhausted.

He'd been pleased to see Emily and Benjamin at the services. They'd both complimented him on his sermon. He was looking forward to marrying them and suspected that with a little nurturing, he could enjoy a good friendship with both of them. They would make a good couple.

Emily hadn't mentioned her sister during their brief discourse as she'd passed through the line, but when Edith took his hand, her eyes brimmed over with tears.

"I'm so happy for Emily and Benjamin. She's just radiant all of the sudden. But you should know that Chelsea is..."

"What has happened? Is she okay?" Ian's heart swelled with concern until it pressed painfully against the walls of his chest.

"She's gone off with him. To where, I don't know. She told me before she left that the wedding wouldnae be occurring and that I was to pass the word along to you."

"I'm so sorry, Edith."

"No outcome would have been a good one when it came to that man, Pastor. He's a bad person, and I wouldnae have wished a man like him for Chelsea's husband under any circumstances."

Ian certainly felt no joy as a result of Greg and Chelsea's decision, but he did feel some sense of relief. Knowing what he knew, he'd not wanted to marry the couple, and so, for now, at least, that problem was resolved. "I'll be praying for the two of them, as I have been all along. Please let me know if there's anything else I can do."

Edith clasped his hand and wiped another round of tears from her cheeks as she walked down the stone pathway towards home.

Ian said a prayer right then and there that God would either work a miracle in Greg's heart or give Chelsea the courage to walk away from the man and reclaim her life. He sighed. It had been a stressful few weeks.

He was doubly glad he'd had the foresight to make reservations for a couple of nights away at a B&B. In an hour or two, he'd be heading to the Cairngorms to enjoy some long, solitary treks through the highlands. The sunshine had brought the wildflowers in the valleys out - the perfect contrast to hard, rocky mountaintops covered with nothing but brittle highland heather and scrubby gorse. Before he came home, he planned to circle round to see his mother. Melinda would be back in Edinburgh by the time he arrived, which didn't bother him in the slightest.

He had one more task to see to before he left. He'd spoken to two or three of the more discreet members of the Kirk Session about the missing artifacts and with their blessing, decided to install his video camera in the courtyard under the flying buttresses. He knew it was probably a futile endeavor and that the man was unlikely to be back, but on the off chance they might catch the thief in action, he felt it would set his mind at ease to try, especially since he was going to be gone.

* * *

The breezes off Loch Awe rippled the grasses in the churchyard as Ian tried to position his video camera to its maximum advantage while taking care to shield it from the elements and hide it from view. He'd thought about placing it inside the kirk, but it seemed like too great an invasion of privacy. People from all over the world dropped by the kirk to say their confessions and pray, and in Ian's humble estimation, he had no right to spy on what was done and said inside the church's walls.

His heart already felt a bit lighter as he locked the doors to the manse and tucked his backpack in the boot of his car. Who knew what the future held for Chelsea and Greg, Emily and Benjamin, or even himself for that matter – except God, of course. But he did know for certain that getting away from Loch Awe for a few days always helped to renew his spirit and sharpen his focus.

He was just about to climb into his car when he spotted another clump of thistles growing beside the main pathway to the kirk. It was half-hidden under a rhododendron bush – maybe he'd missed it. Maybe it had sprung up in the last few days. The sunshine had made everything green and plants and weeds alike were growing quickly.

Well, that was that. This one would have to wait until he got home. He turned and looked up at the outline of St. Conan's turrets and spires.

It was a glorious day, and he intended to go out and enjoy it to the fullest. Abundant life indeed.

Bonus!
First chapter of
the first book in the Wildflowers of Scotland
series.

Wild Rose

Chapter 1

Rose Wilson turned away from the wind that whistled across Loch Awe in a futile attempt to keep her hair from being blown into a tangled knot.

Something nipped at her ankle and she reached down to swat it away. *Pesky midgies.*

Ouch! Her hand scratched against the thorny stem of a thistle. *One more thing.* As if the sticky wicket she'd gotten herself into hadn't already worked her into enough of a dither. She glanced up at the lofty spires of St. Conan's Kirk. If she were at all religious, she might think God was trying to tell her something.

Where could he be? It had been nigh on three years since she'd stood waiting, and waiting, and waiting at Robert's and her favorite restaurant. When he never showed up, she'd been angry – thought he'd gotten too busy at work, forgotten she was waiting, or, worse yet, remembered and blown her off.

How could she have known he was dead?

Here she was again. So it was a kirk and not a restaurant. A man she didn't know all that well instead of her husband. The emotions felt the same. She was peeved. So peeved she could almost forget what it was like to feel abandoned, to hurt so badly she could barely keep her head about her.

She took a deep breath and tried to relax. Would she ever get over being scared that something horrible had happened every time someone was a wee bit tardy?

He was almost an hour later than he'd said he'd be. She peeked through the hedge and tried to see round the bend that led to the village.

What were the odds that two men she was supposed to meet would die en route to their rendezvous point? She paced up and down the path that led to the kirk, squelching her nervous energy only long enough to look at a bee dipping into a rhody that was a lovely shade of lavender. And then, she was back at it, scanning the roadside for Digby's car, checking the time on her mobile every few seconds, and imagining the worst.

She'd been waiting for an hour – plenty long enough for Digby to get there even if he'd been temporarily detained at work, gotten a speeding ticket, or stopped by the mini-mart to buy her flowers. Besides, the man had a mobile.

She clicked hers open and pressed the green button twice. Still no answer.

Where could he be? And why now? Was it because she'd been too intimate with him? Not intimate enough?

"Excuse me, ma'am."

She blinked and looked in the direction of the voice, but the sun was in her eyes, and all she could see was a soft sheen of light backlighting the silhouette of a very tall man. Too tall to be Digby. She raised her hand to her eyes to shade the light but the sun was still blinding, clinging to his head like a halo.

"Forgive me," the man said, just as she saw his collar, the white square gleaming brightly between the black, and thought, *shouldn't it be me saying that?*

"Sorry to intrude," he continued. "I couldn't help noticing that you seem to be looking for someone."

So much for her and Dig having the place to themselves. Of course, as of this moment, there wasn't a "them" anyway, so it mattered little if they had privacy. Besides, she had been going to tell him that they couldn't do it again, that it was too soon, that what had happened shouldn't have. Not yet. That didn't mean she didn't want to be alone with him, to do something. She probably did, eventually. Just not so much, or quite so fast.

"I'm waiting for a friend," she said.

"You've still plenty of time," he said. "Worship doesn't begin for another half hour."

The sun wasn't in his eyes, but behind him, illuminating her face. She knew, even without being able to see his eyes, that he could read hers perfectly.

"I didn't realize..."

"We've a small but active congregation," the man said, extending his hand. "Ian MacCraig. St. Conan's pastor." He nodded at a stone cottage with windows rimmed in tiny stones. It was mostly overgrown with creepers. She had assumed it was unoccupied.

She gave her hand, took his, and was surprised by his warmth. "Rose Wilson." Her hands had been perpetually cold ever since Robert had died. The only reason she'd come to meet Digby in the first place was to get warm. But holding hands with Digby didn't even compare to the heat this man radiated.

"I'm not from Lochawe. Just up for the day from Glasgow."

She turned just enough to get the sun out of her eyes and looked up into his face. And started to melt. Warm times ten. Honest, intelligent eyes, longish hair the color of butterscotch. Wide shoulders perfect for shielding a companion. A genuine, concerned smile tinged with the slightest whisper of what? Guilt? Her mind flipped back a page. Forgive him for what? For startling her? For intruding on her reverie? For being concerned enough to acknowledge her presence? To see if she was in need of someone to talk to?

He had such a beautiful aura about him. So serene. So utterly masculine. She felt like she was in a dream, or starring in a film. She resisted the urge to pinch herself. The vicars she knew were old and gray – most, gone completely bald. This one – Ian, wasn't it? – didn't fit any of the pastoral images she held in her mind.

Pastor Ian's eyes blinked wide open a split second before she felt a movement to her left. A stream of men streaked towards them, guns drawn. She could see them out of the corner of her eye. What the devil was going on?

In the moment it took to comprehend that they were slowly being surrounded by armed constables, her mind, ever agile, jumped to the conclusion that Ian must be a convict, recently escaped. *Oh - my – God.* No doubt "Ian" had killed the real vicar while he slept. It would have been a simple matter from there to don the poor gent's clothes. He was probably planning to take her as a hostage so he could escape across the border to England, make his exit on a ferry, and disappear on the mainland. It was the only explanation she could fathom.

That was when she realized he was still holding her hand, smiling at her with all the sincerity in the world. The man certainly didn't look like a convict. Perhaps he'd come to St. Conan's for sanctuary.

"Step away from the pastor." A voice boomed through a megaphone.

She looked at Ian and dropped his hand, fully expecting the constables to rush him once she'd safely backed away.

Instead, two strong arms wrenched her from behind, pulled her hands behind her back and slapped on a set of cuffs.

"What on earth?" she said, nearly toppling over from the shock of her capture.

Ian looked even more apologetic that he had before, with a little relief mixed in. *Forgive him for what? For this? Had he called the police on her?*

"I've done nothing wrong," she cried. "I'm not sure what's going on here, but there must be some mistake. I'm Rosalie Wilson from Glasgow," she tried to explain when she wasn't struggling to stay on her feet, bucking this way and that as they pulled her over the rough terrain.

"She had nothing to do with the actual theft," the vicar was saying, following close at her side. "She was already gone when her man stole the artifacts."

Her man? Digby? What were they talking about? Digby wouldn't...

"You said she was on the tape," the constable said.

"The earlier part, when they were..." the vicar stammered.

The man holding her cuffs snickered.

Oh, God. They couldn't have a tape of her and Digby. Could they?

"Do you want us to call you a barrister?"

"No," she said, sure of that at least. If Robert's solicitors ever found out, or his sons, or the press...

Oh, God. How mortifying! How could she have? She'd risked Robert's good name, his reputation, and his millions, and for what? To feel a man's touch for a mere five minutes?

A man who appeared to be the ring leader of the hooligans who were herding her towards the car leaned against the vehicle with an amused expression on his face, and looked at her... her... her breasts.

If she'd been blessed with the opportunity to get her hands on Digby at that moment, they'd have had reason to arrest her.

The little weasel! She certainly hadn't meant to get intimate with him when she did, but not because she hadn't trusted him. *My God.* She'd taken up with a common thief, a con man, a criminal.

And the tape. How humiliating! Never in a million years had she ever dreamed... to have had her lowest moment recorded... and seen by who knew how many people.

The vicar rushed alongside her as the constable's men whisked her to the car, with - oh, God - bars on the back windows. "Is there a family member, a friend you'd like me to call?"

She felt her cheeks burning just imagining what the vicar must think of her. "There's no one." Which was a shame. She could certainly have used a hug and a little moral support about then. But she could hardly ring up her mum, or Kelly and Kevin, and tell them she'd been arrested, or that her new boyfriend had turned out to be a criminal, or that she'd been caught on some sort of tape, probably half-naked, her legs spread wide like some common hussy.

"Will you come?" She turned to the vicar and watched as his cheeks flushed even redder.

"I'll get my auto and follow you to the station."

The constable shoved her shoulder into the car and nearly shut her foot in the door in his hurry to lock her in the cramped back seat.

"Good thinking, assuming you're planning to make a confession," he sneered.

"I've done nothing wrong," she said, knowing she had. But not what they thought. She hadn't stolen a thing. What she had done was to throw her whole life down the crapper.

Also from Second Wind Publishing
by Sherrie Hansen

NIGHT & DAY

It's midnight in Minnesota and Jensen Marie Christiansen is dreaming of a rosy future. It's daybreak in Denmark and Anders Westerlund is waking up to a world full of stark realities.

When parchment paper and faded ink meet computer screens and fax machines, the old-fashioned magic of a great-grandmother's letters sets the stage for a steamy Internet romance... and the unraveling of a hundred year-old mystery.

Will fantasy become reality, or will oceans and time keep a second pair of lovers apart?

LOVE NOTES

Hope Anderson's heart is finally starting to thaw. Even Tommy Love's is melting around the edges. They both want Rainbow Lake Lodge. Only one of them can have it. For Hope, recreating the past means new life. It's the only way she can honor her late husband's legacy.

For Tommy Lubinski of Tommy Love and the Love Notes fame, Rainbow Lake means coming home - peace, quiet, seclusion - and a second chance at stardom. Hope is sinking fast, but she'll be fine if she can just keep her head above water until spring. Tommy's troubles run a little deeper, but there's no need to worry for now... Rainbow Lake is frozen solid. Or is it?

STORMY WEATHER - Book 1 of the Maple Valley Trilogy

An ill wind is brewing up a storm and as usual, Rachael Jones is in the middle of the fray. If the local banker succeeds in bulldozing the Victorian houses she's trying to save, she's in for yet another rough time before the skies clear. The only bright spots on the horizon are her friendship with Luke... and her secret rendezvous with Mac...

Is Rachael meant to weather the storm with Luke, who touches her heart and soul so intimately, or with Mac, who knows each sweet secret of her body?

STORMY WEATHER... Stay tuned for the latest forecast!

WATER LILY - Book 2 of the Maple Valley Trilogy

Once upon a very long time ago, Jake Sheffield and Michelle Jones graduated from the same high school. Jake can't wait to take a trip down memory lane at their 20th class reunion. Being with his old friends is like guest starring in a favorite episode of Cheers.

Everybody knows your name. Everybody's glad you came.

The last thing Michelle wants to do is dredge up a lot of old memories and relive a part of her past that wasn't that great in the first place.

Will the murky waters of the past destroy their dreams for the future, or will a water lily rise from the depths and bloom?

MERRY GO ROUND - Book 3 of the Maple Valley Trilogy

Everyone who knows Pastor Trevor, his lovely wife, Tracy, and their three children thinks they're the perfect family. But when Trevor leaves Tracy for a man, Tracy's whole world starts to spin out of control.

The unlikely romance Barclay Alexander III, heir apparent of Alexander Industries, finds with Tracy is the dream that gives him hope. But powerful forces are pulling them apart – her children, his parents, her pride, his honor, the welfare of the entire town.

Heaven only knows if their love was meant to be, or if they will always be on opposite sides of the merry-go-round, riding round and round, never catching up to the other.